THE
RED ROOM
RIDDLE

Books by Scott Corbett

The Case of the Silver Skull

The Mysterious Zetabet

The Red Room Riddle*

Here Lies the Body*

Grave Doubts

Witch Hunt

The Baseball Bargain

Cop's Kid

The Great McGonniggle Rides Shotgun

The Great McGonniggle Switches Pitches

The Hangman's Ghost Trick

The Hockey Trick

The Lemonade Trick

available in paperback

THE
RED ROOM
RIDDLE

A GHOST STORY

by SCOTT CORBETT

Illustrated by Geff Gerlach

Little, Brown and Company
Boston   Toronto   London

ISBN 0-316-15719-8 (HC)
0-316-15754-6 (PB)

LIBRARY OF CONGRESS CATALOG CARD NO. 70-169010

JOY STREET BOOKS ARE PUBLISHED BY
LITTLE, BROWN AND COMPANY (INC.)

HC: 10 9 8 7 6 5
PB: 10 9 8 7 6 5 4 3 2 1

FG

*Published simultaneously in Canada
by Little, Brown & Company (Canada) Limited*

PRINTED IN THE UNITED STATES OF AMERICA

To Treva
With Love

THE
RED ROOM
RIDDLE

1

THE FIRST TIME I saw Bill Slocum I was thinking about Halloween.

I had just watched a man carry a pumpkin into a house across the street, and I thought to myself, "It won't be long now." A shiver of excitement went jiggling down my skinny frame.

While I was enjoying my shiver, the new boy came walking up the street. When I saw him, I thought, gee, it must be windy out. It wasn't, though. It was simply the way he walked, as if he were leaning into a high wind, that made me think so.

He was a big, chunky, clumsy boy with the funniest way of moving I ever saw. He walked slightly sideways, splay-footed, with one shoulder thrust out ahead, leaning forward. His arms were swinging hard, his fists were clenched, and he looked as if he were gritting his teeth. The whole effect was one of ferocious determination.

I watched him turn in at his apartment house a few doors from ours. Then I went out to the kitchen.

"Hey, Mom, I just saw that new kid."

"Did you, Bruce? How does he look?"

"Big."

I wanted to add, "Mean, too," but I didn't. I didn't want her to think I was scared of the way he looked. So instead I said, "He's too big to be in my grade," and was glad of it.

Let me give you an idea of how long ago this was. There was no television. Even radio was just getting started. I still had a crystal set I listened to with earphones. Movies were silent, with the music furnished by a piano player. Most airplanes still had open cockpits and could carry only a pilot and one or two passengers. People drove around in cars that are collectors' items today, cars with things like running boards and isinglass side curtains. Many motorists still had to start their engines with hand cranks.

And Halloween was the most exciting night of the year.

"That big bully *is* in my class!"

When I brought this news home, I was outraged. It was the beginning of dark times for me.

Bill Slocum's specialty was a cruel sneer. When he

4

decided to strike terror into my soul with it, his full upper lip would curl in an alarming way on one side, revealing several blocklike teeth that looked big enough to bite nails in two, while his blue eyes narrowed to slits. Talk about cold and menacing! It looked like the kind of sneer you saw on the faces of the bad guys in Western movies just before they gunned down a poor old rancher.

Well, that was what it was supposed to be.

It was Bill's faithful imitation of the standard Western villain, and was the product of much homework in front of a mirror in the privacy of his room. But I didn't know that then, and it froze my blood.

Bill Slocum did not jump on me and beat me up or anything like that, he simply bullied me in every other way he could think of. And nobody knew it, because he bullied me only when we were alone, on the way home from school. That half mile became longer and longer, until I would sit at my desk just before the final bell and think of home as a dear, distant place I might never see again.

This went on until the day the skinny worm finally turned, when Bill pushed me into one mud puddle too many. I dropped my schoolbook satchel in a red rage and started flogging his face with the most ridiculous roundhouse swings that ever got swung.

You never saw anyone so surprised. And then he started hitting back with a flurry of awkward swings every bit as ridiculous as mine. He was big, but he did

not know any more about fighting than I did. He had never *had* to fight.

Neither of us tried to defend himself, we just hit each other. And after a couple dozen swings we sprang apart like a pair of fighting cocks who were not getting anywhere and had had enough. I picked up my satchel and ran for home, and Bill, if he ran at all, did not run after me.

All that weekend, of course, I wondered what it was going to be like when I saw Bill Slocum Monday morning. He was nowhere in sight when I started down the street heading for school. He seldom got started as early as I did in the morning. But as I was passing his apartment house, the front entrance door banged open and here he came, like maybe he had been watching for me, waiting for me?

"Hey!"

My feet wanted to start running, but something made me stand there and wait for him. Then I saw his right eye. It still had patches of blue-and-yellow skin around it. And he was staring at me in a funny way, without a trace of anger or indignation in either his good eye or his bad one.

"Hey, you sure soaked me one!" he growled. That was our expression in those days, "soaked" instead of "socked."

I had given Bill Slocum a black eye!

My legs were quivering, but I think I managed to look almost stony.

"Well, you didn't have to push me into that mud puddle!"

I did not understand the way he was looking at me at all, and it was a long time before I figured it out, but I believe I understand now. In his crazy, different way of looking at things, I think he was proud of me!

"Well, you gave me a shiner, so we're even," he said. "So now we can be friends."

Darned if he didn't fling his arm around my shoulder and start walking us toward school, all the way with his arm around me, and from that day on we were best friends!

2

OUR NEIGHBORHOOD was a good one to grow up in because there were plenty of places to play. One end of our block was a huge vacant lot, an uncluttered, unlittered open space with a good covering of rough turf, and enough slope to provide some sledding in winter. At the end of the block, Marshall Avenue ran straight up a big hill called Mount Alban. Across the avenue from our vacant lot was a park where there were football fields and baseball diamonds laid out.

We were always busy doing something outdoors, except when rain drove us inside. There were enough boys in the neighborhood to make up a pretty good gang, enough to get up a game of something whenever we wanted one. But a lot of the time Bill and I would just drift around together and take things as they came.

There was one night in the year when we were allowed to run loose after dark. In our calendar, as I said, that was the most exciting night of the year. We looked forward to Halloween for weeks, planning where we would go and what we would do.

In those days, it was all tricks. When we went out on Halloween, we considered the entire world as our enemy. We were not vandals, though; we were not out to destroy property. We were out to bedevil people. And we did.

Of course, we knew Halloween was a night when witches and ghosts and goblins were supposed to be abroad, but that stuff was for little kids. We enjoyed cutting faces in pumpkins to put in our windows with candles burning inside the pumpkins, but when Halloween came we were too busy with our own pranks to worry about what the spirit world might be doing.

At least, that was true the first year Bill and I went Halloweening. The second year was different.

Bill was a great reader, though not very good in school. He was constantly reading up on one subject or another, and as it happened, about a month or so before Halloween he got interested in the supernatural.

Also as usual, Bill was after facts. He seldom read stories. The books he read were the kind called nonfiction, the kind that are supposed to tell you what's real and what's true. Facts.

In that way we made a good combination, because I

was always reading stories. I got my facts from Bill, but when I sat down to read a book, and I loved to read as much as he did, I wanted to read a good story.

So when Bill started reading books that explained why people sometimes believed in ghosts, I began to read ghost stories.

We went to our nearest branch of the public library every week and absolutely pillaged the place, carrying home as many books as they would let us take. During the latter part of September and all of October we read almost nothing but books about ghosts and other supernatural stuff, everything the library could produce.

At first, when I started bringing home nothing but ghost stories, my mother was concerned, and not sure she should allow such goings-on.

"You've got a wild enough imagination as it is, without filling your head with ghost stories," she declared, but my father said, "Oh, let him have his fun. Don't worry, Bill Slocum will keep him straightened out."

"But you know how high-strung Bruce is," said my mother, using a favorite expression of hers that always made me think of someone hanging by his thumbs. "Well, all right, but just let me catch you having any nightmares, young man, and that will be the end of your ghost stories."

I grinned at her and said, "Heck, I've never slept better than lately."

Our library had a good children's room, but it was not big enough to hold Bill when he got going on a

11

special subject. He read the adult books, too, struggling with the big words, getting as much out of them as he could. The librarians were so impressed with his interest and determination they usually let him take out any book he wanted. And they let me take out books that were not in the children's section, too, when I started nosing around in the adult stacks and discovered some ghost stories there.

My father was right about Bill. His interest in the supernatural was a negative one. He said he did not believe for one minute there were any such things as ghosts, but what he wanted to figure out was all the ways a lot of dumb people had been fooled into thinking they had seen ghosts. He wanted to know about all the tricks and hocus-pocus and monkey business that had been involved. I would retell the stories I read, and he would laugh at them and draw on what he had read to explain how they could have happened.

"What our neighborhood needs is a good haunted house, so we could do our own research," Bill said one day when we were walking home from the library.

"Well, the only house I know that's supposed to be haunted is up on Mount Alban," I told him.

"No kidding? Say, they ought to have high-class ghosts up there," Bill wisecracked, because the top of Mount Alban was the fanciest residential district in town.

"Virgil Higbee got me to walk up with him once to have a look at it," I went on. "His dad had been talking about it the night before. He said something terrible was supposed to have happened there long ago. As near as Mr. Higbee could remember, there was some story about a baby's body that was found buried in the garden, all chopped up. Anyway, the house has been empty and boarded up for umpteen years, and it just sits there, because Virgil says there was some trouble about the estate and the case has been in the courts for years."

Here I was parroting Virgil, who was always parroting his father, who was a lawyer.

"Well, what did you see when you got there?"

"Not much. It's a big old place, but it's way back from the street wth a high stone wall in front of it. Looked pretty spooky, though, what we could see of it through the driveway gates."

"Hmm. Well, someday we'll have to walk up there and take a look. Maybe we can climb over the wall."

"The heck we can. The wall's got broken glass all over the top of it, set in cement."

That was a few days before Halloween. The afternoon of Halloween, when we got home from school, we decided to take my football and walk over to the park fields to practice drop-kicking field goals. The drop-kick was still used then, and was a lot more fun than this business of having somebody hold the ball on the ground for you. At least I thought so, because I was pretty good at it, for a lightweight.

That year Halloween came at the perfect time, on a

Friday. It was great to think of not having to go to school the next morning. But there was always something to worry about. The only cloud on our horizon was just that, a cloud. In fact, lots of them. As we walked down through the backyards between the small apartment houses that lined our block and were crossing the vacant lot, the thing that had us worried was the weather. It had been cloudy all day, and now the sky was growing darker and darker. Was it going to start raining and spoil our big night?

Bill gave the sky a dirty look.

"Well, I'm going out tonight whether it rains or not. It can rain cats and dogs; I'll still be there."

"Me, too," I said, "but darn it, it won't be as much fun if it rains."

"Well, it better not, that's all!" warned Bill, bullying whatever rain gods might exist.

We plodded on across the vacant lot, with tufts of stiff, dead grass crackling under our heels, and a mummified leaf or two fluttering down from a few gnarled trees that survived out in the middle of the lot, and I suppose it was the combination of the general gloom and the dark sky and Halloween that made Bill think of the house up on Mount Alban.

"Hey, I've got an idea! This is the perfect day to go take a look at that haunted house. To heck with kicking goals, let's walk up there."

Offhand it sounded like a lot of effort for nothing. The only time I had ever set foot in the fanciest part of

14

Mount Alban was that time with Virgil Higbee. A neighborhood like that did not have much to offer as far as kids were concerned. All I could call up now in my mind's eye was a vague picture of quiet, tree-lined, winding streets with high stone walls on both sides and an occasional glimpse of an imposing mansion through wrought-iron gates. From our neighborhood at the base of the hill it had been a long, steep climb up there. Virgil's so-called haunted house had hardly been worth the trip.

So I raised objections.

"Aw, it's too far. And we couldn't see anything when we got there. Besides, I don't think I could even find it. The streets go every which way. When I went with Virgil he knew the way, so I didn't pay much attention to how we went."

"So what? When we get up there we can ask somebody."

I knew Bill well enough by then to know what he was like when he got an idea into his head. His mind was made up; there was no use trying to argue with him. But naturally I argued anyway.

"Listen, you're crazy if you think we're going to ask anybody anything up there. There won't be anyone walking around the streets in that neighborhood. It's just a bunch of great big houses and they're all a mile apart and they all have stone walls in front of them. We'd be lucky if the police didn't come along and ask us what we were doing there."

Of course, that set Bill off.

"What do you mean? It's a free country! We've got as much right to walk around in a ritzy neighborhood as anybody else. You just let some old cop get smart with us and he'll hear from my father!"

A breeze sent a chill whisper through the tall grass around us, and the twisted limbs of the trees trembled against a background of ominous gray sky. In spite of myself I began to think that having another look at that haunted house might be exciting. But just to be contrary, I had to think up some new objections.

"Listen, I don't want to lug my football all the way up there and back."

"Okay, we'll hide it somewhere."

"Nothing doing! Somebody might find it."

"Aw, who's going to find it out here?"

"You never know."

"Then I'll carry it. My gosh, you'd think it weighed a ton, the way you talk!"

"Aw, it's not that . . ." I grumbled, my objections becoming even feebler.

"Then let's go."

I sighed heavily.

"Well," I said, "I just hope I can find the darned old place!"

3

I KNEW the house we were looking for was somewhere near the top of Mount Alban and at least three or four blocks in from Marshall Avenue. Virgil had walked me up there from the other end of our block, and if anything we had borne to the right rather than the left.

"Why didn't you think of this before we left home?" I complained as we toiled up the hill. "We could have gone the way Virgil and I went, and maybe I would have remembered how to get there."

"You said you didn't pay any attention, so what's the difference?"

"It's twice as far this way. Besides, then I wouldn't have had to carry my football."

I had not exaggerated the way the streets twisted around up on Mount Alban. When we turned off Marshall Avenue near the top of the hill we left behind the standard squared-off city blocks and entered a residential neighborhood where the tree-lined streets curved in elegant sweeps and were called Drives. Fillmore Drive, Addison Drive, names like that.

All sounds of traffic and street life soon faded away behind us. As I had predicted, no one but us was using the sidewalks. For a long time we did not see so much as a car, until finally a Pierce-Arrow limousine rolled by with a chauffeur at the wheel and one little old lady in the back seat. We walked along in silence past haughty stone walls relieved only by the occasional iron gates of driveways. Glimpses of velvety lawns, formal gardens, rows of French windows, and the stone or brick façades of spacious mansions seldom betrayed the slightest sign of life, any more than did the streets themselves.

When a corner finally came into sight around a bend ahead of us, I had no idea where I was, so I took refuge in sarcasm.

"Well, the house is around here somewhere. Just ask anybody. That's what you said we could do."

"Aw, shut up. *Somebody* will come along." Bill pointed to a mailbox on the corner. "They must at least come out to mail letters."

"They probably send the butler to do that."

"Okay, what's wrong with a butler? He could tell us."

"Fine, then all we've got to do is hang around the mailbox till a butler comes out with a letter."

During our walk up the hill the weather had not

improved. The sky had grown so dismal it was like dusk under the tattered trees. We were a long way from home if it began to rain. But just as I was considering that depressing possibility, and was getting ready to annoy Bill by mentioning it, a mail truck rattled round the corner and stopped beside the mailbox. Bill was having his usual luck. He ran on ahead, calling to the mailman as he climbed out of the truck to make his collection.

"Hey, mister, can you tell us how to — to —"

His feet and his tongue both faltered to a stop. He turned and glared at me in embarrassment.

"What's it called, Bruce?"

I saw his problem, but I had no answer for it. Until that moment neither of us had stopped to consider what we would say if we asked someone for directions.

I fumbled for words.

"We're, uh, we're looking for that house that's supposed to be haunted. The one that's all boarded up, and, uh —"

As luck would have it, of all the mailmen who might have come along we had to get one who was a real card. He stopped in the middle of shaking his keys apart at the end of his key chain, picking out the one to open the mailbox with, and grinned as he eyed us, especially me.

"What are you boys doing, looking for a Halloween thrill? You going to take those spooks on for a game of tackle? Maybe you'd better make it a game of touch."

Sometimes the only thing to do about grown-ups' wit

is to endure it, so we smiled sickly smiles and Bill said, "We just want to have a look at the house."

"Well, you can have a look, all right, but don't think you're going to take yourself on a tour of the place, because it's all shut up," said the mailman. "Stay on this street till you come to Beardsley Drive, then turn left. It's the second house down."

We thanked him and hurried on. Naturally I couldn't resist rubbing in what the mailman had told us.

"You see? You heard what he said. It's all shut up."

"I heard him."

"Well, he ought to know."

"We'll see."

Sometimes Bill gave me a big pain, the way he wouldn't take anybody else's word for something till he had found out for himself. But I didn't argue with him any more, because another corner had come into sight and the street sign said BEARDSLEY DRIVE.

A high stone wall turned the corner with us and continued along beside us. Through the gates of a driveway we could see a large house that looked much like all the others we had passed, but a moment later, behind some tall trees, I could see one corner of the top floor and mansard roof of the house we were looking for. Not only was it the second house from the corner, its windows were boarded up and the boards were gray with age.

I put out my arm to stop Bill.

"Look, there it is."

"I got eyes, dopey, I see it," growled Bill. Then he added with satisfaction, "It's really big, all right."

Before long we reached the point where the first house's stone wall ended and the second house's wall began. The walls were the same height but, as I had remembered, the top of the wall around the vacant house was covered with jagged pieces of broken glass set into cement. A sparse straggle of ivy on the wall looked as pathetic as the last few hairs on a bald man's pate.

"You can bet nobody's going to get in *there*," I insisted.

"Who says so? Look, there's a door in the wall."

The door was a solid, heavy wooden one, the wood dark and dull, with a few flakes of rusty-brownish paint still sticking to it.

"Okay, there's a door," I said, "but you can bet it's blocked up on the other side."

Bill, of course, had to stop and give it a push for himself. And wouldn't you know it? There was a crotchety squeak, and it swung in an inch or two. Bill was always getting breaks like that, and each one made him more cocksure than ever. He looked around at me with an arrogant grin.

"Can't get in, huh?"

"Listen, are you crazy? You want to wind up in real trouble? You better stay out of there, you got no business in there!" I yammered, taking out my annoyance by turning self-righteous. Bill's grin continued to tease me.

"No harm in just taking a look," he said, and put his beefy shoulder against the door. This time, creaking again in a tone of querulous complaint, it opened enough for him to stick his head through. Left outside with the rest of him, I glanced nervously up and down the street. There was not a soul in sight, nor a sign of life anywhere, nor a sound of it.

Bill pulled his head out with a pleased look on his face.

"Boy, is it a mess in there! Regular jungle. I'm going in."

"Well, I'm not!"

"Okay, be a sissy," he sneered, and gave the door one more shove. He slipped inside and left me standing on the sidewalk with my head jerking from side to side as my eyes darted up and down the street, expecting a police car to come screaming up out of nowhere. But no policeman appeared, nor anybody else. There was just me in the gloom under the trees, alone in an emptiness that seemed suddenly full of whispers. I swallowed my pride and slipped through the doorway.

Bill was standing to one side with his arms folded, waiting.

"I knew you'd come," he gloated, and stepped over to push the door closed. I looked at the heavy iron bolt on the back and frowned uneasily.

"Why would they leave the bolt open on this door?"

"Who?"

"Well, whoever looks after the place. Somebody must. Maybe somebody went out this way, somebody who'll be back."

"Aw, stop worrying so much. There's plenty of places to hide, if we have to, if anybody comes. Let's take a look while the looking's good." Bill waved his hand at the tangle of bushes and weeds that all but choked out the path leading from the door through what must have once been well-tended grounds. "What did I tell you? Regular jungle. Come on, let's go see the house."

I had burned my bridges behind me, I had committed myself to the crime of trespassing, and now the excitement caught hold of me. It was all I could do not to rush on ahead. I wanted to see everything we could as fast as we could and get out of there. Get out of there before anyone came, before it grew any darker.

"Okay, let's go."

"We'll follow this path," said Bill, and led the way.

4

TO FOLLOW THE PATH we had to push between bushes that grew on each side and almost met in the center. We had not gone far, however, before the path both opened up and closed in ahead of us. That is to say, it ran into what looked like a tunnel built of jack-straws, a tunnel through a thicket. We pulled up short in front of the dark opening.

"What the dickens is this?"

"Some kind of trellis." Bill peered inside. "All the bushes and stuff have grown clear across the top of it."

Here and there we could see bits of the lattice framework, most of it cracked and split, still in place. The strips of wood looked like the gray bones of some large, badly fractured skeleton. We could see through the passageway to the other end, but in that dim light it seemed a great distance.

For me the prospect was scary but irresistible. Once we were through we would surely be near the house, near enough for a really close look. With a small flare-up of courage I had not expected, helped no doubt by a sharp desire to surprise Bill, I said, "Come on!" Crouching to avoid the stray tendrils and twigs that hung down or poked their way into the tunnel-like passageway, I took the lead.

"Hey!" As he came along behind me, the sound of Bill's astonishment was sweet to my ears. But then he startled me with a different cry.

"Ow!"

I looked back.

"What's wrong?"

He was holding his cheek.

"Something scratched me."

We struggled out of the far end of the passageway into the open.

"A thorn," declared Bill. "Some of these vines have prickers on them."

He took his hand away, and I saw a long red scratch on his right cheek. He asked, "Is it bleeding?"

"No, I don't think so."

"Well, the heck with it," he said, and stared around us with challenging eyes. We were in a level area where traces of gravel paths made a faint pattern through a weedy tangle under towering trees. To our right, so massive and tall it seemed to lean toward us, stood the house.

It was three stories high. Above the ground floor all the windows were boarded up. On the side facing us, fire had blackened most of the red bricks. Something was missing; the scar on the wall was obvious. Between two pairs of windows with several small panes broken was a door whose sill was at least three feet above the ground, which meant it must have once led to some steps, or a porch. Rotting wisps of drapes still hung in some of the windows, but beyond them, in that dim light, all was lost in shadows.

I stood and stared at the grisly bulk of the house, spellbound. I was not disappointed. It looked authentically evil. No sound however frightful that burst through those shattered windows, no shriek or groan, would have surprised me. Even Bill was impressed into silence, though I could see he was not as chilled by the atmosphere of the house as I was. But you have to remember that while he had been reading the nonfiction books, I had been reading the stories. When I glanced sideways at the overgrown garden, my imagination scooped small, shallow graves in a dozen likely locations.

In the stillness that enveloped us and held us motionless, we suddenly heard a sound. The sound, when it came, was neither a shriek nor a groan, and came not from the house but from a thicket close beside us.

It was a panting sound, and then a sniffing sound.

Sniffing and panting, and the padding of paws. Some creature was close by, and in my frame of mind it could have been anything. This time Bill was scared, too, because whatever was there must be a Fact, possibly a dangerous one.

"He! he! he!"

A second sound came from behind us. A high-pitched, mocking laugh made us whirl around. With his hands in the pockets of gray knickers and a gray cap cocked over one of his glittering eyes, a short, spindly boy about our own age stood with his small feet planted wide apart as he grinned at our pale faces.

"I know what you're looking for," he said.

Almost at once, Bill started to get some of his color back. In fact, it flooded into his face and turned it an angry red.

"Who are you?" he wanted to know.

"I'm Jamie Bly, and I snuck in here, too, but I'm not scared," said the boy, still making fun of us. His glance flicked past us toward the house. "Even if there *were* any ghosts in there, they wouldn't scare *me*," he bragged. "I'll bet you're afraid to go in."

Bill was in no mood to take a lot of guff from a boy half his size who had made him jump. He narrowed his eyes and gave Jamie the full benefit of his special sneer.

"Listen, you little twirp, you'd better shut up if you know what's good for you," he snarled in a hoarse voice. "Maybe what you need is a push in the face!"

27

He took a step toward Jamie. As he did, Jamie gave a sharp whistle.

"Here, Major!"

Shouldering his way out of the thicket, panting and sniffing, came the biggest, ugliest bulldog we had ever seen. Bill froze in his tracks, face-to-face with a large and definitely dangerous Fact, while Jamie laughed at him again.

"What's the matter? You're not scared of old Major, are you? He won't hurt you, unless you ask for it."

Glaring speechlessly, Bill eased back alongside me. Major gave us a ferocious look, with his huge, thick tongue hanging out over his steamshovel bucket of a lower jaw, and then waddled over and sat down beside Jamie.

"What's your name?" Jamie asked Bill.

"Pudding Tane. Ask me again and I'll tell you the same," retorted Bill, giving him a fast answer that was still going the rounds in those days.

Jamie's mouth thinned out coldly.

"Ha, ha," he said, and repeated more sharply, "What's your name?"

Major stood up, cleared his throat, and gazed with pointed attention at Bill's right leg.

"Bill Slocum," Bill decided abruptly, and I stammered, "B-Bruce Crowell!" before Jamie had done more than jab his beady glance my way.

"Okay, now let's see who's scared," said Jamie. "Let's go take a look in there."

Here was something Bill could handle, and by now even to me the house seemed tame alongside this nasty little kid and his bulldog. Ghosts were something I didn't really believe in, but Major was big enough to tear my leg off.

"Okay, let's go," snapped Bill, and we turned and headed briskly for the house. Jamie skipped up alongside us, grinning, while Major padded along behind, and when we reached the side of the house it was Jamie who climbed up with surprising agility onto the doorsill and pulled himself erect by grabbing the doorknob.

"Stay there, Major," he said to the dog, and to us, "Come on," as he twisted the knob and pushed the door open with the assurance of someone who had done it before. While Jamie waited just inside, Bill climbed up with much less ease than Jamie had displayed, for all his spindly build. I tossed Bill the football, climbed up, and took it back from him. In an odd way it felt good to be holding it, as though it were a kind of protection, a talisman which by its own leathery reality would ward off evil spirits.

Once we had scrambled up, we stepped into a scene about as dismal and dreary as could be imagined, because the inside of the house was well along toward becoming a wreck. The walls were covered with speckly black blotches of mildew. Many of the floorboards had buckled into long, narrow mounds. Some had broken loose and bowed up at the ends. In the room we had entered, warped and sagging bookshelves lined the

30

walls. Beyond it a huge room stretched into shadows. There was not a stick of furniture anywhere, nor anything else to give the rooms a hint of life.

Jamie glanced around with an air of malicious merriment, jerked his head at us, and picked his way across the uneven floorboards to the doorway that opened into the larger room. With the floors setting up an unholy creaking din under our feet at each step we took, we came along cautiously behind him. My heart was pounding, but Jamie's jaunty assurance drew me on. All the stories I had read about deserted, haunted houses were whirling through my mind, but none of them matched up with what we were seeing. This house was so desolate it was not hard to feel that even the ghosts had deserted it.

From the far side of the huge room we had now entered, a wide staircase led to the upper stories. Signaling over his shoulder, Jamie pattered nimbly across the barren waste of time-blasted flooring, making straight for the staircase. Over my shoulder I stared back at Bill. His lower jaw, jammed forward stubbornly, looked like an imitation of Major's. His shoulder was pushed forward as though it had a chip on it. He was glaring defiantly at Jamie's narrow back.

The stairs sloped away from the wall at an alarming angle. Even though they were massive, they hardly looked safe. But Jamie started up them without the slightest hesitation, again with that air of familiarity that made me feel sure he had been inside before. By now I was numb; I was operating like a robot. With a queasy feeling I followed him, comforted only by the sense of Bill's being close behind me. As each step took us higher, the light from the windows grew more distant and dim. By the time we had made the turn on the stairs and reached the second-floor landing, we were nearly in darkness. A long corridor ahead of us blurred into a dark gray square that might or might not have been the far end of it. Beside us a second flight of stairs, narrower now, slanted up into blackness. And Jamie seemed to have every intention of going on.

"Hey!" Bill spoke with something in between a low growl and a hoarse whisper. Jamie stopped, and I could imagine just how much his complacent smirk rasped on Bill's nerves.

"What's the matter?" he murmured. "Are you yellow?"

This was a new insult — "yellow" — and for devotees of Western films, one not to be taken lightly.

"Shut up, you!" hissed Bill, shoving his face close to Jamie's. "I'm not yellow, but I'm not crazy, either. I'm not going up there without a flashlight. You can break your dumb neck if you want to."

Needless to say, Bill had my support. How this clash of wills would have worked out I don't know, because at that instant something else ended the argument.

Downstairs, somewhere, a door was opened. A doorknob rattled, a door scraped the floor, and we heard footsteps, slow and shuffling.

5

IF JAMIE BLY had looked as frightened as I felt at that moment, I don't know what I might have done. But he merely put a finger to thin lips puckered into a sly smile. He murmured two words.

"The caretaker."

The *caretaker*? At first it seemed preposterous to suggest anyone was taking care of such a house, a house that was going to wrack and ruin. But then I remembered I myself had suggested there might be some such person around when I saw the gate had been left unbolted. Despite its condition, somebody would have to keep an eye on the place. Besides, Jamie seemed to know what he was talking about.

"Don't worry, he's half blind and hard of hearing," he added in a whisper. "Get down and watch!"

A half-blind man keeping an eye on things — that seemed fitting enough. Jamie dropped flat on his stomach behind the bannister, and we hastily flattened ourselves beside him. With my arm over my football alongside me and my heart banging against the dusty floorboards I listened to the shuffling footsteps and stared goggle-eyed between two ornately carved balusters at the room below.

The footsteps came from the part of the house opposite to the side we had entered, and were accompanied by the querulous grumblings of someone talking to himself. Through a wide arch to the left came a scarecrow of a man in baggy, dirt-colored work clothes and a moth-eaten felt hat with the brim drooping in a tired, wavy line. He was carrying a broken ax handle, clutched like a club.

He came to a slow, shuffling stop near the foot of the staircase and peered around in every direction with eyes that were fierce and blank. I was terrified when he glared straight up at us, but it was plain from the way his glance kept moving he could not see us. Suddenly he brandished the ax handle and raised his voice in a badgered whine.

"Where are you, Jamie Bly? I know you're in here again! You get out of here and take that brute of a dog with you, or I'll fix you good!"

Of course, none of us made a sound. I don't know whether anyone else was holding his breath, but *I* certainly was. I rolled my eyes sideways enough to glimpse

Jamie's face. His lips were parted unpleasantly, and he was watching the old man with a sort of bored contempt, as though he would have hated him if it had been worth the trouble.

The caretaker's voice subsided into a half-intelligible mumble, and he resumed his slow patrol across the room. When he had disappeared through the door at the far end, Bill muttered, "What'll we do now? How long's he going to hang around?"

"He'll come back through in a minute."

"What if he sees Major out there?"

"Don't worry about that. Old Major's too smart for him."

Jamie seemed to be right about this, because we heard no further outbursts from the old man, and a moment later he returned and recrossed the room. He was still mumbling uncomplimentary things about Jamie, but this time he did not stop at the stairs. His footsteps faded, a door scraped the floor, then silence filled the house again.

Bill was on his feet.

"Let's get out of here."

"What's your hurry? He's gone."

"He may not stay gone. Come on, Bruce."

Once again Bill had my backing. I was right behind him on the stairs. Jamie made scornful noises, but there was no stopping us, so he followed along. The slanted stair treads creaked and rattled so loudly under our feet it seemed impossible anyone could be too deaf to hear us, and my nervous glance saw in every shadowy corner a lair for unimaginable attackers. Never had Bill seemed heavier-footed than he did at that moment, picking his way deliberately across the huge room, defying the house to make him hurry. But at last we reached the smaller room and the door to the garden, and then a dire premonition sent my heart plunging: I was sure the caretaker had locked the door.

Bill took hold of the knob and turned it. My premonition was false. The door was not locked, probably no longer had a workable lock at all. He pulled the door open and we stared out into the gloom of the weed-choked garden. Major was nowhere in sight. Bill jumped down clumsily and heavily. I sailed out like a grasshopper. Jamie calmly pulled the door closed and dropped easily to the ground.

A sudden challenge startled us.

"*Here* y'are!"

The old caretaker careened violently into sight around the corner of the house. He still carried the ax handle and looked crazy enough to beat our brains out with it. Weedy grass swished around our flying feet as we broke into a mad run, racing toward the dark hole in the tangled shrubbery. I heard Jamie cry, "Stop that, Major! Come!" and I saw the big dog in a corner of the garden as I rushed past. He was digging, he had dug a shallow hole, and something stuck up out of it that was like a sliver of old ivory or a small, age-yellowed bone, something I caught only a blurred glimpse of before I plunged into the trellised tunnel behind Bill, with my head down and my breath coming hard. With my football clutched in my arms I must have looked like somebody going for a touchdown.

We flashed through the darkness of the tight passageway, fought our way through the tangle of bushes beyond it, and reached the splintery door in the wall. Bill put all his beef into a yank that dragged it open. We burst into the quiet street.

"He! he! he!"

Jamie was close behind us, enjoying our fright. Major wallowed along at his heels as they came through the doorway.

"Hold it!" called Jamie. "That old stiff can't run this far, so take it easy!"

"Go soak your head!" Bill snarled over his shoulder, and we did not slow down till we had turned the corner and were out of sight of the house. Only then did we stop, winded, and bend double as we tried to puff some breath back into our lungs. Jamie had stayed with us relentlessly. Now he stopped alongside us and pointed at me.

"If you want to see a ghost, get a load of him," he wisecracked to Bill. "He's pale enough to be one."

"Shut up!" was the best retort I could provide at such a moment, wheezing it out in a feeble gasp.

"You guys make me laugh," said Jamie. "I could have told you you wouldn't see any ghosts in that old dump."

Bill's eyes blazed at him in a way that should have made him glad he had Major along.

"Never mind the ghosts — you could have told us that crazy old nut of a caretaker was there!"

"Aw, he's nothing to worry about. The only reason I sneak in is to have fun with him."

"If he gets the police after you, maybe you won't talk so big!"

"I'm not worried about him. He'll be out of a job next week anyway, because I know something he doesn't even know. Next week they're going to start tearing it down."

"That house?"

"Yes."

"You're nuts. It's all tied up in the courts."

"Not anymore. It's been settled," said Jamie, as cocksure as if he had been a lawyer himself.

"Aw, how do you know?"

"I know, so forget it." Jamie's sly eyes measured us thoughtfully, and abruptly he changed the subject. "You guys going Halloweening tonight?"

We glowered at him. In the gathering dusk some streetlights had come on. One of them, behind Jamie and across the street, threw his shadow long and thin across the sidewalk in front of us.

"What if we are?" said Bill.

Jamie chuckled.

"It'll be pretty tame," he predicted, and the glance Bill and I automatically exchanged was an admission that this, at least, was a point we could not argue with. Our usual Halloween adventures were not likely to equal what we had just been through. Even the present moment, alone on that deathly quiet Mount Alban roadway with Jamie and Major, was eerier than the familiar streets of our own neighborhood could ever hope to be. Jamie watched us, and all at once his manner changed. He cocked his head to one side and studied us with intense and unsmiling earnestness.

"Listen, if you really want to see some ghosts, just say so, and I'll show you some," he said. "You want to?"

The matter-of-fact way he asked us was like asking if we wanted to see a movie, or a litter of new puppies. The ridiculousness of his question made Bill stare at him and then snort.

"Sure, why not?" he jeered.

"Okay, then. You meet me tonight, and you'll see some real ghosts."

"Ha! Who are you kidding?"

"I'm not kidding."

"Aw, go home and call the doctor! You're nutty! There's no such thing as real ghosts, and if you think so, you're nutty as a jaybird."

"No, I'm not."

Jamie looked at us with all the confidence in the world, and said something that nearly dropped us in our tracks.

"I know there are ghosts," he said, "because I live with them."

6

NOW, IF it had been Virgil Higbee who said a thing like that, we would have known what to do. We would have had a good laugh. Virgil was always coming up with wild stories, and we knew how to take them. But Jamie's casual confidence gave his words a force that left us staring at him while we wondered if we had heard what we thought we heard.

"My house is full of ghosts," he went on, still in that same conversational tone, "and if you don't believe me, meet me tonight and I'll show you."

There were only two ways of looking at it. Either this little twirp was really nutty, or he was the smoothest liar we had ever met. Too smooth, in fact. This time it was I who thought of a retort.

"Listen, I don't believe there's any ghosts in your

house, because if there were you'd be scared, but you talk as if it wasn't anything."

Jamie laughed at my logic.

"Why should I be scared? I'm used to them, and they don't hurt me none."

Now Bill came up with something.

"I suppose your folks are used to them, too!"

"They don't know anything about them," replied Jamie.

Bill put his head back and hooted.

"What? You trying to tell me you see a bunch of ghosts running around in your house and they *don't?*"

Instead of saying anything back, Jamie merely taunted Bill with that smart-aleck grin of his. But Bill kept right after him.

"Well, if *they* can't see them, then *we* wouldn't, because they're all in your head!"

When it came to getting under Jamie's skin Bill might as well have been working on a rhinoceros. Jamie only laughed.

"Don't worry," he said, "you'll see them, all right."

I never saw Bill look more frustrated, nor felt more so myself. Here was this pint-sized squirt, as skinny as I was and sawed-off besides, making one farfetched claim after another and expecting us to fall for them. You wanted to grab him and shake him till you shook the nonsense out of him and he admitted he was making it all up . . . but there sat Major, panting, with about a yard of mottled red tongue hanging out of that mammoth mouth of his. It was a situation you could stand just so much of. Bill jerked his head at me with a huge display of disgust.

"Come on, Bruce, we're wasting time talking to this loony! Let's go home!"

"Suits me!" And we turned on our heels to walk away.

"Meet me at seven thirty at the corner of Fillmore Drive and Harkins Way," said Jamie.

We glared back over our shoulders and Bill shouted, "Go soak your head!"

Jamie made no move, but simply watched us stamp off down the quiet street into the dusk. Major, I was relieved to see, made no move, either, but only sat watching us and scratching his fat, white belly with one short hind leg.

Then Jamie called one last order after us.

"Be there!"

"Go jump in the lake!" I yelled in a voice so shrill it cracked on me, and we turned our backs on him for good. The street curved away under the dreary arch of wintry brown trees, and when I glanced back once more over my shoulder he was out of sight.

"That kid's nutty as a fruitcake," growled Bill.

"He's a liar and a show-off," I snapped. "He likes to hear himself talk. I'll bet if he ever even *thought* he saw a ghost he'd jump out of his skin."

"Fillmore Drive! Why, that's at least a couple of blocks farther up, and I never even heard of Harkins

43

Way. The day we waste Halloween to walk all the way up there! . . ."

"You said it!" I agreed, and glanced down irritably at my football. "We've wasted enough time on him already."

But I knew that was not true, of course. Whatever we had done, we had not wasted our time, if experiences count for anything. It was true that already, now that our scare was over, my memory was turning the old caretaker into a comic figure, a slapstick menace; but there were other aspects of the experience that brushed across my mind like icy fingers . . .

"Did you see Major when we started running, Bill?"

"No. Why?"

"He was digging a hole, and Jamie told him to stop."

"So what?"

"Well, there was a piece of stuff sticking out of the ground where he was digging. I was running too fast to get a good look at it, but . . . it looked like a bone. A little bone."

Bill stared at me.

"You're kidding."

"No, I saw it."

"You mean, you *think* you saw it," snorted Bill, disgusted with me. "Heck, anything you saw right then you'd make something out of."

"I don't care, I saw it," I said, turning stubborn.

"Well, I didn't," said Bill, as if that settled it. "For Pete's sake, stop being dumb! Unless we snuck back in

44

there and took a good look, how could you be sure what it was you saw when you were running lickety-split?"

"I'm not going back to look," I assured him. "Besides, if Jamie's right they'll start tearing down the place next week, and then nobody will be able to get in there to look, anyway."

"Aw, Jamie's probably full of hooey about that, too!" growled Bill. I dropped the subject, but it refused to drop me. I still saw Major's thick paws gouging the black earth, and a yellowish sliver of something leaning sideways in the hole with the tilt of a disturbed tombstone in a country graveyard. . . . We hurried on silently, each wrestling with his own welter of thoughts. As the familiar, everyday traffic flow of Marshall Avenue came into sight, I blurted a thought out loud.

"He wouldn't be there, anyway," I muttered, and Bill's quick response showed how our minds had been on the same track.

"You bet he wouldn't. And even if he was, I wouldn't go."

"Me neither."

Yet this solid agreement left us in a surprisingly bad temper, which the weather speedily made even worse, because it started to sprinkle.

"Oh, for Pete's sake! Now I suppose it's going to rain and spoil our whole night!"

Our spirits hit a new low as we jogged down the hill with home still a long way to go. Before we got there, however, the sprinkle had stopped, and we began to hope against hope again. We agreed to meet as soon as we could after dinner, which meant about seven o'clock, because my mother would never let me go out immediately after dinner on Halloween. She had a theory that if I started out right away on a full stomach all the running around and excitement would make me sick. Mothers are always full of crazy ideas like that. I couldn't talk any sense into her, no matter how hard I tried.

"And I want you to wear your slicker," she added that night.

"Aw-w-w-w!"

"I won't have you catching your death of cold, not even for Halloween. Besides, what's wrong with a slicker? You'll look that much more like a spook."

"Aw, who can run with a slicker on?"

"You can. I've seen you."

"Well, but not as good as without one. Gee whiz!"

As usual, I lost that argument. When I left the house, I had my slicker and rain hat on, with a resentful frown under the hat.

Bill was waiting outside. His apparel and expression matched mine.

"Your mother made you wear yours, too, huh?" I noted.

"Don't you worry; when we get going we'll stash them somewhere."

"But darn it, it still feels like it *is* going to rain!" I pointed out, much as I hated to admit it.

"Well, anyway, let's get going. What'll we do first?"

"Heck, I don't know." My heart wasn't in it. "Listen, did you tell your folks about Jamie?"

"No, did you?"

"No."

Our glances slid together and apart again, sharing guilt.

"I've been thinking," I admitted.

"That darn Jamie!" complained Bill.

I nodded glumly. Curiosity was a pain in the neck sometimes, the way it wouldn't let you be.

"He gives me the willies," I said. "I wish we'd never met him."

"So do I."

But we had. We were trapped, and we knew it.

"For two cents I'd *walk* up there," Bill blustered in a tentative way, feeling me out, "just to show him up . . ."

"So would I . . ."

The trouble was, if we didn't walk up there to see if he really was waiting on the corner, we would always wonder about him.

"If we hurried, I guess we could be back here in time to have *some* fun, anyway," Bill decided, and that was that. We melted into the darkness, but not in our customary Halloween direction.

47

7

TWENTY MINUTES LATER we were walking along Fillmore Drive. We had been following its curves and bends for a long time without coming to any Harkins Way.

"He probably made up the name himself!" said Bill. Our anticipation of the helpless fury we would very soon be feeling was growing with every apparently fruitless step we took. The same fear had been nagging both of us all the way, the fear that Jamie would not show up and thus make fools of us for coming. Now we had begun to fear that even the corner itself would not show up. Fillmore Drive wound down over the slope of Mount Alban and left the great mansions behind, entering a district where the houses were still large, with sizable front yards, but not in the mansion class.

"Well, let's go to the next corner, whatever it is, and then let's head back before we waste any more time!" I suggested, angrily determined to salvage what we could of a badly botched Halloween.

"Okay with me. But if I ever see that little twirp again — without that big mutt! . . ."

But then at the next corner Fillmore Drive came to an end in a T intersection with another street, and the other street was Harkins Way.

The corner was there, but Jamie was not.

Of course we were instantly furious. We glowered around us, and Bill fumed, "I *knew* he wouldn't be here!"

I clutched at a straw.

"Well, I don't think it's seven thirty yet. We better wait till it is."

"Well, okay, but I'm not waiting one minute after!" declared Bill, though how we would know when seven thirty had come and gone was a good question, since neither of us had a watch.

Harkins Way was a quiet, backwater type of street, where the houses lost all pretensions of being upper-crust and became plain and ordinary. If there were any kids in the neighborhood, they were not in evidence, and neither was anyone else. During the time we stood there, not so much as one car went past. While our precious Halloween was slipping by, here we were, wasting it on a deserted street corner waiting for a nutty kid we hated who was not even going to show up.

Next it began to rain. Not sprinkle. Rain.

Now we were really angry. Now Bill, if he'd had a nail with him, could have bitten it in two with those horse-sized teeth of his. We huddled under the inadequate shelter of a bare-limbed elm and waited, first on one foot and then the other, while flash floods streamed down our slickers.

"This is the worst Halloween I ever had!" Bill announced.

"This is the worst Halloween *anyone* ever had!" I declared, and went straight to Headquarters with my complaints. Darn it, God! I whined silently — an unusual way to begin a prayer, perhaps, but that was the way I felt — Darn it, God, Thou hast all year to make it rain, why dost Thou have to make it rain on Halloween? . . . You will notice I had at least picked up some proper prayer-type pronouns and verbs in Sunday School.

I was genuinely miserable. It was not like a ball game; there were no rain checks for Halloween. You could not have a doubleheader next year. It was now or never, and now it looked like never, as far as this year was concerned. I continued my prayer. "And why didst Thou make us meet that nutty kid and get us stuck up here on a corner in the middle of nowhere?"

No answer. The rain continued to beat down on us. Bill gave the tree a kick, just to get the kick out of his system, and said, "Aw, let's go."

And then, as we were turning to leave, here came Jamie through the pouring rain, strolling along as though it were the nicest fall evening of the year. He had on a raincoat and his same gray cap. Padding along beside him, also seeming to ignore the rain, was Major.

A moment before, we had been furious because we had not found Jamie waiting. We had felt like gullible fools. But now that he had come, we felt even worse. Now that it was too late to do anything about it, we discovered how humiliating it was to let Jamie find us waiting and know we had been suckers enough to come. Had we spotted him soon enough, I think our impulse would have been to hide, to watch *him* wait around, and never let him know we had come at all. But by the time we noticed him he was only half a block away and we were sure he had already seen us.

The sight of him stirred us both into a rapid change of thinking. Seconds earlier Bill had been simmering with frustration and defeat. Now he was instantly alert and planning our campaign strategy.

"Judas Priest, here he comes!" he muttered. "Now, listen, no matter what he has up his sleeve, just remember one thing — it's all a lot of hocus-pocus, just hocus-pocus. Don't forget that."

Hocus-pocus, hocus-pocus. I nodded grim agreement, and we turned to watch Jamie approach. Bill handled the greetings.

"Well, it's about time!" he said.

"What do you mean?" said Jamie. "It's seven thirty, and that's when I told you to be here. Come on, I'll take you to my house."

His glance flickered over us as though we were trophies. He turned to lead the way.

"We weren't going to come, except we knew it was going to rain and spoil everything anyway," Bill claimed, but that only got him another mocking look. This annoyed him so much he tried his special sneer again, and he was never sneerier. "Well, you better show us some ghosts, if you know what's good for you," he warned, using a favorite threat of his. But once again he was wasting his efforts. Jamie showed not the slightest concern.

"You wait," he said.

We had expected a short walk to one of the houses close by, but after a block or so he turned right and led us back in more or less the direction we had come. I say more or less, because the way the streets curved it was hard to be sure. He pattered along at a quick pace with Major snuffling along beside him, and after a while he turned again, and then again, until we might as well have been blindfolded for all we could tell about where we were. The only thing we could be certain about was that we were back in the highfalutin part of Mount Alban, back among the high and mighty stone walls and the lordly mansions.

"Say, where are you taking us?" Bill demanded finally. "Don't try to tell me you live around here!"

"You'll see," said Jamie. "My house is as big as that old dump we were in this afternoon. It's as big, and as — well, as *everything*."

"I'll bet. Listen, stop stalling!"

"We're almost there."

We were passing a long stretch of high stone wall covered with ivy whose wet leaves gleamed blackly in the rain. Ahead of us there was a break in the ivy around an archway in the wall, and set into it was a door, a solid wooden door painted a dark, rich red, with a rounded top to fit the arch. Like the ivy, it glistened darkly in the dim light of a distant streetlamp. Jamie stopped and gave us a glance that was malicious with anticipation of our surprise.

"Home, sweet home," he said, and pushed the door open, changing the dark-red outline into a pitch-black opening.

It was obvious he expected us to be startled by the door in the wall, and we were, but we were also immediately suspicious. There were probably dozens of such doors in the miles of walls in that neighborhood. I had noticed two or three myself when we were looking for the haunted house that afternoon. It would be just like Jamie to lead us to one he knew was not locked and say that was where he lived. Did he expect us to take one look and turn tail, and give him a good laugh as we tore away down the street?

"Home, sweet home, huh?" scoffed Bill. "Sure, and I live in the White House!"

"I told you my house was as big as that other one," said Jamie. "You see if it isn't. Come on, what are you worrying about? You afraid of a garden? Follow me. Besides, old Major's here to protect you."

Up to that moment we had certainly not thought of Major in terms of protection. Motioning to us, Jamie strolled through the arch, and after giving us an inquiring look that appeared almost friendly, Major went bowlegging in behind him.

Watching Major, I knew my comfortable suspicions were false. Boys like Jamie might bluff, but dogs did not. A dog does not trot through a strange doorway the way Major did, as though he owned the place. Jamie really did live here. The thought was profoundly disturbing. I looked at Bill and his expression alarmed me, even though I felt a sickly admiration for the set of his jaw. Bill was going in.

"I didn't walk my feet off and waste Halloween just to chicken out now," he muttered, and with that I made my move. I might be scared, but I was more scared of being left alone. I darted through the arch a step ahead of him.

I stopped almost as abruptly as I had started, for once inside I could scarcely see my hand in front of my face, it was so dark. What light there was from the

55

street narrowed to a slit and disappeared as the door swung shut behind us. We heard the soft thud of its closing, and Jamie's satisfied chuckle. I could feel gravel under my feet, and as my eyes began to get used to the darkness I could see the path stretching ahead of us like a hazy gray ribbon, closely bordered by bushes and trees.

A few yards ahead I could make out the dark outlines of an arbor.

"Where's the house?" Bill demanded in a loud voice. "I don't see any house."

"Don't you worry, it's there. Follow me and Major."

We could see Jamie as a small, dark blur now, starting on ahead of us, and could hear Major's broad paws scuffing on the gravel. As we picked our way along behind them we even began to see signs of light through the trees ahead of us and off to the right.

"At least we'll get in out of this darn rain," muttered Bill, coming along behind me. His tone of voice had noticeably relaxed. A glimpse of light made all the difference. Now that we knew we were close to a house with Jamie's father and mother and other everyday things inside, such as nice bright electric lights, my own courage made a spectacular comeback. I stopped worrying and began wondering. Was Jamie really a rich kid, after all? One of those rich kids who don't have any friends because they always act nasty and superior toward ordinary kids like us? I had seen enough movies to know what rich kids were like! Well, we could handle one of them. Whatever hocus-pocus Jamie Bly might have in mind, he was going to be surprised. I was sure Bill was thinking the same things and feeling the same way, and so eager was I to show Jamie his tricks could not scare us that I did not even hesitate when the path led us into the gloom of the long, vine-covered arbor.

Walking into the arbor was like walking into a tunnel. Suddenly the darkness was total and absolute. The path could have turned into a pit, for all we could see of it anymore. But I could still hear Major scrabbling along, so I kept going, even though I did slide my feet ahead and feel around a little as I took each step.

Wssssssssssssssssssh!

Something icy cold whished past my right ear with a whispery hissing sound, and almost instantly Bill yelled, "Hey! Something hit me!"

From somewhere up ahead of us, Jamie spoke sharply in a strange, shrill voice.

"Stop that! Don't be in such a hurry!"

His words made no sense to me.

Whom was he talking to?

It didn't sound as if he were talking to us.

All I wanted to do was get out of that arbor. I shot out of the far end of it with such a rush I nearly stumbled over Major, who wheeled out of my way with a startled growl. Bill came walking out behind me holding his cheek. And I mean walking, not running. Walking in his usual splay-footed, shoulder-forward way. It

57

took a lot of stubborn belief in his own ideas, and disbelief in anything else, to do that.

"I wasn't hurrying!" he squawked indignantly. He, at least, thought Jamie had been talking to him. "I was just walking along, and something scratched me!"

Jamie's voice was silky smooth. "Don't you know enough to keep away from thorns in a rose arbor?"

"Thorns, my eye! Thorns don't make funny noises. You pulled some kind of trick back there, didn't you? You've got a peashooter, I'll bet." And then, of all things, Bill's voice took on a wheedling tone. "Come on, Jamie! Tell us how you did it, and I won't hold it against you, honest!"

The trick of it. That was what Bill was always after, the trick of it. Of all the kids I ever knew, only Bill Slocum would have been able to take things the way he took them that night. He was not even scared, he was so sure Jamie Bly had worked some slick trick on us. But Jamie laughed, and gave us back some of our own medicine.

"Funny noises? If you heard any funny noises, they must be in your head. You better see a doctor," he said. "Come on, we'll go in through the porch door."

Rain was coming down in sheets now, making it hard to see much, but what I could see looked good to me after that black moment in the arbor. We were in an open space, with the neat, fussy, geometrical outlines of flower beds all around us among gravel paths, and the towering bulk of the house was close by. Light

58

glowed in a subdued way through the windows of a big, glassed-in side porch. Jamie and Major walked off ahead of us and were swallowed up in rain before they had gone thirty feet. The rain was pounding down so hard we could barely hear Jamie's high, thin voice when he called back to us, "Come *on!*"

Bill took his hand away from his cheek.

"Hey, Bruce, is it bleeding?"

"For crying out loud, how can I tell?" I said, blinking up at him in the downpour. "I can hardly see at all in this rain!"

I was amazed, though, by what I could see of Bill's expression. He had a savage grin on his face, as if he were actually enjoying himself.

"I'll find out how he worked it, you wait and see!" he promised. "Maybe we're going to have some fun tonight after all! Let's go, before we get drowned."

I was so astonished I said, "Okay, let's go."

We put our heads down and ran for the house.

8

FOR THAT MATTER, it did not take much nerve to decide to head for the house, because it was either that or turn around and leave. The house at least offered lights and the company of grown-ups, even if they turned out to be as weird as their son. Leaving would have meant a return trip through that arbor.

Three steps led up to an entrance at the back end of the glassed-in porch. Jamie was holding the door open for us. Though the porch was unlighted, the soft glow that came from the house through the inside windows was enough to give me an impression of lots of wicker furniture and plant stands, a low table or two, and a scattering of rag rugs on the tiled floor. Jamie took off his raincoat and cap and threw them on a wicker armchair.

"Leave your stuff here."

We piled our wet things on top of his and followed him into a room with bookshelves from floor to ceiling, all filled with dead-looking sets of books in dreary brown leather bindings. Overstuffed chairs covered with pebbly black leather squatted here and there. In one corner stood a vast flat-topped desk with intricate carved paneling along its front and sides.

Oddly enough for a library, there was not a reading lamp in the whole room. The only light, the light we had seen from outside, came from an oil lamp sitting in the middle of the desk. It was a hurricane lamp, the kind with a tall glass chimney. Bill stared at it, and looked around the room.

"How come the lamp? Is your electricity off?"

Jamie grinned as though he had been waiting for this.

"We don't use electricity," he said. "We like gaslight and oil lamps."

Well, in those days there were still plenty of homes in America that did not have electricity, but they were mostly in the country. There were still a few streets in our city that had gas streetlights, with lamplighters who came around every night carrying a small ladder on which they climbed up to light the wicks. But few houses, except in the poor parts of town, were without electricity. Yet here was a big house, a mansion, with oil lamps and gaslight! What kind of people were

Jamie's folks, anyway? Or was he only fooling? Was this another of his crazy jokes?

And as for his family, where were they? The house was as still as a tomb.

"Where's your father and mother?" I asked, though I was no longer sure I was anxious to meet them.

Jamie's dark eyes flickered slyly.

"Are you nuts? Do you think I'd bring you home to show you some ghosts if they were here? They're not home tonight. I knew they wouldn't be, that's why I said to meet me. Do you think I'd want them here, and have you running to them pretty soon with a lot of wild stories? Not on your tintype!"

Jamie had tricked us neatly. He had let us think what we wanted to think, but now I realized that not once had he said his family would be home.

His remarks made sense from his standpoint, but they left me with a sudden sinking feeling. It was one thing to come in expecting to find other people present, another thing to learn we were alone in the house; one thing to be alone in some modest home, like my family's five-room apartment, another thing to feel the bulk and distances of a mansion around us.

Almost as if they were passing before my eyes in a veiled jumble, I sensed the endless maze of sitting rooms and bedrooms and spare rooms and forgotten rooms and closets and attics and basements and dark corners that waited around us and above us and below us in that huge, silent house. And for that matter, was it truly silent, or did it only seem so because of the noise of the storm outside and of the rain that was lashing the windows?

"You're pretty sneaky, you are!" Bill told Jamie. Jamie's deceit had shaken him up, too. Bill might not scare easily, but even so he had been going along on the assumption he would find Mr. and Mrs. Bly sitting in their living room. Like me, he had foreseen an evening of sneaking around in the more distant parts of a normal-sized house (Jamie doing his best to produce spooky effects and make us think we Heard Something or Saw Something), and having Jamie's best efforts spoiled by his mother calling up the stairs, "Jamie, what are you boys doing up there? Bring your friends down; I have some nice cider and cookies for you."

The usual. But instead of that, we had this great, still, strange house with a single oil lamp between us and total darkness, and Jamie Bly standing there watching us with hard eyes, and a bulldog sitting in front of him dangling a tongue like a red necktie from a monstrous, saber-toothed jaw.

"You wait here," said Jamie. "I'll light some more lamps, so we can see to go upstairs. My old man's stingy about light. He never leaves more than one lamp burning down here when they go out for the evening. I'll be back in a minute."

Jamie disappeared through a wide doorway into the murky darkness of another room, whose size we could sense more than see. Major followed, his toenails clicking on the floor in the spaces between carpets. A match scratched and flared, and Jamie reappeared distantly in the midst of a huge living room, lighting a lamp whose glow brought plush-covered sofas and armchairs, ornate mahogany side tables, and tall, glass-fronted cabinets out of the shadows. It was all heavy, dark, cheerless furniture, and Jamie looked small and lost in the midst of it.

He blew out the match and moved out of sight again on the far side of the room. Bill stared after him with scornful disapproval.

"If you ask me, his folks would have to be as nutty as he is to leave a kid like him alone in a house." Then Bill gave me a nasty start as he added, "But I don't believe he *is* alone."

I gulped.

"Wh-what do you mean, Bill?"

"Well, anyone with a house this size must have some help working for them."

"Oh!"

I felt foolish. For a moment I had misunderstood. But naturally Bill would not have meant —

"I'll bet they've got a cook and a maid, maybe two," he went on. "Maybe even a butler."

"Then where are they? I wish someone would turn up; I don't like this place, it gives me the willies," I yammered nervously. "For two cents I'd get out of here."

"What? Just when it's starting to be fun? No, sir. No,

sir-ee!" said Bill, tromping on my craven impulse before I could even get it going. "We're not turning tail now. That little monkey thinks he's going to have a good laugh at us, but we're going to fool him. Remember what I said. Hocus-pocus!"

Once more Bill astounded me. He wasn't scared at all! He was enjoying himself! He was not without imagination, but his kind of imagination was different from mine. It held no place for any things that could not be explained, or rather for the possibility that there were such things. As I stared at him, my eye was caught by a red mark on his cheek. A second red mark.

"Say, something *did* scratch you! You've got another scratch beside the one you got this afternoon!"

"Yeah?" Bill touched the place and frowned, though not without a certain admiration. "That kid must have been watching us the whole time this afternoon, and figured it would be a neat trick to make me think I got scratched again the same way in a place that was like the other place. I'll bet he did have a peashooter or something —"

"Huh! Whatever went by me must have been frozen solid, then, because it felt ice-cold."

"Well, yes, that's so. Made a funny noise, too. Listen, we've got to be on our toes with this kid; he may have plenty of tricks up his sleeve," said Bill, welcoming the challenge. "He's got a great setup to work with here. This place is laid out so much like that old haunted house he naturally figures it will scare us half to death all by itself. I'll bet that's what gave him the idea."

As he concluded this analysis, Bill began to bustle busily around the room.

"While we've got a chance," he said, "let's find out where the light switch is."

"What light switch?" I cried hopefully.

He gave me a disgusted look.

"You didn't believe that hokum he handed out about the lights, did you? Nobody has a house like this without electricity, not in this daynage," said Bill, making "day and age" sound like one word. "No, sir, not in this daynage," he repeated as he poked about the room looking for light switches or disguised lamps or some sort of concealed lighting. I joined him in the hunt, eager to discover an unobtrusive button somewhere that would suddenly fill the room with good old no-nonsense electric light and throw a monkey wrench into Jamie's buildup with the oil lamps.

We searched the walls without success. But Bill gave ground hard.

"Well, maybe this room *doesn't* have any, for some crazy reason, but I'll bet you their living room has. Come on, let's go in there —"

As he turned, his hand shot out to grab my arm. With his other hand he pointed.

An old woman had come into the vast living room so quietly we had not heard her. She was walking toward the lamp Jamie had lit. She was wearing a maid's black uniform with a white lace collar and cuffs, and she had a maid's cap perched on her white hair.

"What did I tell you?" Bill murmured, pleased to be proven right about the help. As she bent over the lamp, frowning and muttering to herself, he stepped across the room toward the doorway and called to her.

"Er — hello, ma'am, can you tell me —"

The living room went dark.

She had blown out the lamp. But despite the darkness we could still pick out the white trim of her uniform as she went silently out of sight.

"Hey, ma'am! . . . What's the matter with her, is she deaf?" Bill wondered. But then he glanced around at me and grinned. "I'll bet she's going to give Master Jamie an earful for fooling with that lamp."

"The way she acted, you'd think she didn't even see you," I said. "Maybe she's nearsighted and hard of hearing both. She looked pretty old."

"Well, come on, let's not miss the fun. I'd like to catch Jamie getting told off. That would just about ruin his whole act!"

Bill picked up the hurricane lamp, eager to follow the maid. The lamp was heavy enough so that he had to steady it with both hands, and he had to walk slowly to keep the flame burning upright inside the tall glass chimney. We crossed the thick carpets of the living room, threading our way through the clusters of sofas and armchairs and ponderous tables, and saw that a wide archway, with fancy iron grille gates pushed back against the wall on either side, led into a dining room. The archway was at the nearest corner of the room, which stretched away to our left, with a table in the center of it long enough to seat at least twenty people.

The dining room was dark, but at the far end of the long room was a door. The bottom edge of the door showed a slit of light.

We looked at it silently. Then Bill set the lamp down on the dinner table and jerked his head at me. I followed him to the door. It was a swinging door, the kind people often have between dining rooms and kitchens. Bill pushed it open.

The door opened into a serving pantry. Beyond the pantry was a kitchen. That was where the light was coming from. The door between the pantry and the kitchen was open.

On the kitchen table was another hurricane lamp. In front of it, with his back to us, Jamie Bly stood hunched over the table, his arms moving busily.

Silhouetted against the lamplight, he looked like some pint-sized sorcerer hard at work on a feat of black magic, his movements furtive and quick. My imagination was off and running, conjuring up all sorts of horrid possibilities as to what devilish surprise Jamie might be preparing for us.

Hearing the door open, he turned around.

You would never guess what he was doing.

9

YOU WOULD NEVER guess in a million years.

Jamie was making a peanut-butter sandwich.

He grinned, not the least embarrassed at having us catch him at it.

"I'm hungry," he said. "Ate early. Want some?"

Ordinarily we would not have turned down peanut-butter sandwiches anywhere at any time. But there was something about Jamie that made our skin crawl at the thought of eating his food.

"Not me," I said.

"Me neither," said Bill. "Listen, stop stalling, will you? We ain't got all night. Either show us these ghosts of yours or don't."

Jamie finished making his sandwich and bit into it greedily.

"Enty uh ime," he said in standard peanut-butter language. Without anything sticking to the roof of his mouth, the words would obviously have come out, "Plenty of time." Bill glanced around the kitchen. Nobody else was there but Major, lapping water noisily from a dog dish in a corner.

"Where's that maid we saw?"

"Whah may?" Jamie swallowed, and spoke more clearly. "What maid?"

"She blew out that lamp you lit in the living room, then she came this way."

"That was old Henrietta. She's always blowing out lamps. She's worse than anybody about wasting light."

"Where did she go?"

"Oh, she's around." Jamie picked up the kitchen lamp with his free hand. "Let's go."

He led the way through the pantry and pushed open the door into the dining room.

The dining room was dark. The lamp Bill had brought from the library was still on the table, but it was out.

"Hey!" cried Bill. "What happened to my lamp?"

"What lamp?"

"That one. I brought it with us from the library, and now it's not lit."

"Oh." Jamie chuckled. "That's Henrietta again."

"Listen, don't give me that," snapped Bill. "We just came through this room after her and she wasn't here."

Jamie looked down at Major and made a contemptuous gesture in Bill's direction with his peanut-butter sandwich.

"Mr. Smarty knows it all," he said, and walked on through the dining room. Since the only light was leaving with him, I felt like staying close, but Bill stopped me. Stopped me and held on to me while Jamie and Major and the light all turned the corner and disappeared into the living room.

Bill had never been fiercer or more determined to do things his way. Even in the dark I could tell this was no movie sneer, this was the real thing. He was mad. He burst out at me in a whisper that was raspy with exasperation.

"Stop acting that way!"

"Wh-what way?"

"You look scared stiff! You going to let that twirp scare you?"

"*He's* not what's scaring me —"

"Listen, you sissy, he doesn't fool *me*! I know what's going on. I just asked him those questions to see what he'd say." Bill was like a general who had called up his reserves and was spoiling for a fight. "He's got the hired help working with him to play tricks on us!"

"What? Aw, now, listen, Bill, grown-ups wouldn't —"

"Don't tell me! A rat like Jamie could make servants do anything. I got it all figured out. Remember that movie we saw about the rich kid who was such a rotten little sneak? Remember how he spied on the servants

71

and found out secrets about them, and then they had to do anything he said?"

"Well, yes, but —"

"Well, that's it! I'll bet you anything!"

"But — how did our lamp get blown out? Henrietta wasn't here when we —"

"That's easy! She went through the kitchen and circled around while we were talking to Jamie. Now, listen! From now on, let's fool him. No matter what he says or does, no matter what happens, don't say anything about it. Don't give him the satisfaction. Just keep telling yourself, It's a bunch of hocus-pocus, hocus-pocus, that's all, because it is! Don't let him —"

Light glowed again in the archway at the far end of the dining room. Jamie peered around the corner at us.

"Well, are you coming or not?" he asked. "I thought you were in such an all-fired hurry."

"Sure, we're coming," growled Bill. He gave my arm a hard squeeze to remind me to get that look off my face, and we joined Jamie and Major.

"First we'll go upstairs to the Red Room," said Jamie, and I could feel That Look stiffen my face again. The Red Room! I didn't like the sound of it. But as Jamie headed for the stairs, Bill gave me an elbow in the ribs and a warning glare, and I marched forward on prickly legs. Hocus-pocus, hocus-pocus!

The staircase was wide enough and grand enough to be in a palace, the way it looked to me. Its polished wooden treads were so dark they were almost black, and gleamed dully in the lamplight. As we mounted the stairs, the treads creaked and crackled in a dismal chorus, and I shied like a startled pony when I happened to glance sideways and notice the enormous tapestry on the wall beside us.

There seemed to be about an acre of it. It was so large the figures in it were life-size, and right away I knew what the tapestry's picture was all about. A Sunday School story that had made an impression on me was the one about the time King Herod told his soldiers to go out and kill all the children who were two years old or under. The Slaughter of the Innocents, it was called.

In the trembling light of the lamp Jamie was carrying, the soldiers seemed to be actually moving, sticking their swords into babies and chopping them up while their mothers screamed. I certainly did not think much of his family's taste in tapestries. No wonder they had a kid like him!

Halfway up, the staircase made a right-angle turn. When we reached the halfway landing I saw something up ahead of us that made me forget the tapestry. In the upstairs hallway a gas jet was burning inside a glass globe held by a wall bracket.

"I lit a light so you wouldn't be afraid to come up," said Jamie, giving us one of his special looks over his shoulder. Bill and I glanced at each other. Who was he trying to fool? Even though we had stopped to talk, there had not been time enough for him to go all the

way upstairs, climb up on a chair, light the gas, and come down again. Somebody else had lit it, someone who was already upstairs. Probably that poor old Henrietta, I decided.

We climbed the rest of the stairs. At the top a long hallway stretched into increasing gloom ahead of us. I expected Jamie to lead us that way, but instead he turned and stopped at the foot of another flight of stairs, a narrower one that led to still another floor. His eyes glistened with a sick sort of pleasure.

"Didn't I tell you my house has everything that old dump had?" he asked. "You wouldn't go on upstairs there, but we have a light here, so you don't have to worry."

Bill gave him a long look, then stared up the stairs. They were not dark. There was a light up there somewhere, too. He stuck out his chest, jerked his head at me, and said, "Let's go. I want to see this."

There was no longer any feeling in my legs, but somehow they took me up behind him, with Jamie giggling softly as he followed, and Major scrabbling along heavily at his heels.

On the third floor, another long hall stretched in both directions. On the wall, a gaslight like the one below was lighted. We reached the landing just in time to catch a glimpse of someone far down the hall to the left, but it was not Henrietta. It was a man. And almost at once he slipped through a side doorway and disappeared.

At that point Bill broke his own rule about making comments. In a sarcastic voice he asked, "Who's that, the butler?"

Jamie acted genuinely surprised.

"How did you know?" he asked. "Most butlers haven't worn clothes like that for a hundred years."

"I don't know anything about his clothes, I just know a butler when I see one," boasted Bill, as though this one were not the first butler he had ever seen except in the movies.

Once again Jamie bounced a remark off Major, who had sat down panting beside him.

"You hear that, Major? Mr. Smarty knows all about butlers. He! he! he!"

That high-pitched laugh of his, about as full of fun as a groan in a graveyard, stirred up eerie, hollow echoes in the hallway as we walked past one closed door after another, coming ever closer to the end of the hall.

Jamie stopped in front of the last door on the left. He looked at us, and his upper lip lifted just enough to show a row of small, even teeth in a tight, expectant grin.

"Okay," he said, "here's the Red Room."

10

WITH THAT, Bill really let him have it. He put on a big display of scorn to show Jamie he was not fooled by what was going on.

"Boy! I'd hate to work for your family, with *you* here," he declared. "You sure must have the goods on these people, the way you can make them run around doing things like this."

Jamie acted puzzled.

"Like what?"

"Like hiding in rooms to scare kids. You want us to walk in there so that butler guy can jump out of a closet moaning and groaning —"

"Jason?" Jamie hooted at the idea. He seemed to find it especially funny. He laughed and shook his head. "Jason! That's a good one. He didn't go in here. You can bet Jason won't be in the Red Room if he can help it. He never stays in the Red Room, he doesn't like it. He has to go in there sometimes, but he doesn't like it, not one bit. You'd hear moaning and groaning, all right!"

I had never listened to such nutty talk in all my life, and there was more of it. Jamie snickered as he went on to add, "Jason's *afraid* of the Red Room. Believe it or not, he's afraid of it!" he said, and pushed the door open.

He did not turn the knob, he just pushed. The door swung open, slowly, with a soft scraping sound that was like a sigh. The rays of the lamp he was carrying threw a wider and wider band of light through the doorway as he stepped forward, and we saw why he called it the Red Room.

Everything in the large bedroom was some shade of red. None of it was light red, either. Mostly it was a dark, blood red, from the wallpaper and the close-drawn drapes to the canopy hanging around the tall four-poster bed. An upholstered armchair was covered with scarlet satin. A scarlet runner lay across the top of a red dressing table. A picture frame was trimmed with scarlet velvet, and the picture . . . Even across the room I could see what it was. It was an engraving of the same subject as the tapestry beside the staircase. The Slaughter of the Innocents.

Jamie walked in and set the lamp down on the dressing table. When I hesitated on the threshold, Bill nudged me forward and followed me in. Jamie looked

78

up at the ceiling with chuckling satisfaction. Even the ceiling was painted blood red, but it was shiny and sticky-looking, as if the paint had never dried properly.

Bill took everything in with his head cocked at a pugnacious angle, and managed to remember something he had read that came in handy.

"What's this supposed to be, a warship deck?" he jeered valiantly. "They used to paint —"

"That's right," said Jamie, finishing the story for him without taking his eyes off the ceiling, "on the old wooden ships they used to paint the decks red, so when the battle started and men started getting blown to smithereens, the blood wouldn't show. How do you like that ceiling?"

Bill stared at it, and kept trying.

"Well, if you ask me, you got a leak in your roof. It looks wet."

"It ought to," said Jamie, and suddenly swept his eyes around the room with a look of vicious glee. He threw his arms wide. "This room's the best one in the whole house. It's got everything. It's even got a secret staircase."

"Aw, come on!" scoffed Bill.

"You don't think so? You're so smart, look at the fireplace and see if you can find it."

We both stared at the fireplace, with its great andirons standing on the hearth, not brass ones but iron ones painted red, and with a red marble mantelpiece above it, and I thought of some of the stories I had read.

Was there really a secret opening in the wall with a staircase behind it, or was Jamie only pretending there was?

His small, thin face was twitching with private pleasure as he goaded us.

"Go on, take a good look. It won't bite."

"Aw, shut up," snapped Bill, and stepped closer with two of his splay-footed strides. I edged forward beside him.

The door closed softly behind us. I whirled around, startled. Jamie was gone.

"Hey!"

I ran to the door. On our side, instead of a knob, the door had a fancy wrought-iron handle. I grabbed it with both hands, twisting it down and tugging with all my might. The door would not open.

"It's locked!"

Bill gave it a try, yanking on the handle in a fury, but he could not even make the door rattle, much less pull it open.

"He! he! he! Go on, let's see how good you are," Jamie urged in a venomous, giggling voice. "Let's see you find your way out. And you'd better not waste time, or you'll see more than you bargained for."

We called him a few choice names that only brought on another of those giggles. Then Bill stood back from the door, blew out his breath like an aroused bull, and stared around the room.

"Well, at least he left the lamp, the little wart!"

He glared at my pale face and gave me a low-voiced reminder.

"Hocus-pocus, hocus-pocus! That's all it is, a lot of hocus-pocus!"

He turned back to the door and yelled at Jamie again.

"Are you going to open this door, or am I going to start kicking out the windows?"

Outside in the hallway, Jamie laughed softly.

"What windows?" he asked, and then we could hear his footsteps and the click of Major's toenails going off down the hall. I rushed across the room to the window drapes and pulled them apart.

Behind them there was nothing but wall.

I stared around at Bill with panic screaming in my mind, trying to take over. The whole room was abnormal, but a bedroom without a window . . . My throat felt thick, as though I were suffocating. Something dreadful had happened in this red room, and would happen again.

"That kid's crazy!" I whispered. "He's crazy! And this house is —"

"Shut up!" Bill cut me off as though he did not want to hear what I might say, did not want to be swept along by my growing sense of real and hideous danger. "He may be crazy, but he meant it about the fireplace," he said, and turned back to it. "There must be a staircase behind it. Come on, let's find it!"

Something to do! Nothing else could have staved off my panic. The prospect of doing something made all the difference. Suddenly I was thinking once again, thinking about the stories I had read, and about decorations around fireplaces, with designs like the scrolls and rosettes on the iron molding around this one. If Bill was right and Jamie was telling the truth, then there must be something concealed in that design that would open a secret panel, or door, or something. I skittered over beside Bill and began pawing every projection of the surface. There was a rosette at each corner near the top, with petals radiating from buttonlike centers. Eagerly I pressed on the left-hand one, but it was hard and unyielding. Bill watched me, and pressed on the other one.

His face lit up.

"Hey! It went in —"

Both of us stumbled backward in a hurry, because the fireplace was moving. Slowly and smoothly, without a sound, the whole ponderous mass was swinging sideways into the room.

"Look! There *is* a staircase!"

Bill nodded, immensely pleased with himself.

"I knew it!" he said. "I knew it!"

The iron staircase was narrow, and twisted straight down out of sight into darkness. A spiral staircase. It hardly looked inviting. I spoke my doubts in a low voice.

"How do we know this isn't some other trick? Something worse?"

Bill glanced around the Red Room.

"You want to stay here?"

"No!"

"Then let's go."

"Okay. You want to carry the lamp?"

Bill shook his head.

"Won't need it."

"*What?*"

If he had looked pleased with himself before, he looked enchanted now.

"I figured we might want this, so I borrowed it from my father," he said, and pulled out of his pocket a small flashlight. "It's a real good one. He'd kill me if he was home and knew I took it," he added with a grim chuckle.

He switched it on, and its small, bright beam was like a shot in the arm to me. Electric light! I had never known how good it could look till then. That shaft of modern-day light, sharp and unwavering, seemed to cut through the shadowy dangers I had felt all around us and shatter them to bits in the corners of the room. A moment ago I had been ready to whimper. Now I almost crowed as that flashlight put me back in touch with reality.

"Hey, that's great! Let's go!"

Cocky now, Bill led the way, with me close behind. Very close, for all my new-found courage.

Circular staircases are not something you run down two steps at a time. The little triangular metal treads make for tricky footing, especially when the staircase is tight and narrow, as this one was. You keep turning and turning round a central pole, and after two or three turns you are halfway dizzy. We had barely started down, however, when a sound made us stop.

The door of the Red Room was being opened. We could hear its soft sigh as it brushed the floor. Bill switched off the flashlight. Looking back up the staircase, I could not see into the room — we were too far around the bend for that — but I could see the glow of lamplight reflected from the curve of the staircase's iron wall.

Soft footsteps pattered across the room and stopped. The wall went black. While we held our breath in utter darkness, the footsteps pattered out of the room, and the door softly closed.

Bill switched on his flashlight. We stared at each other.

"Old Henrietta again."

"I think she *is* crazy," I said. "They're all crazy!"

"Crazy or not, she couldn't miss seeing a hole in the wall. She'll tell Jamie we found the staircase. Come on."

And what then? Like cold fingers on my backbone, a new fear sent a shiver through me. What would we find at the bottom of the circular staircase? So eager had I been to escape from that grisly Red Room I had not stopped to wonder where the staircase might take us. Not till now. I reached for Bill's shoulder.

"Wait! We're nuts to go down here. It's just what he

wants us to do. So let's fool him — let's go back! I'll bet old Henrietta didn't lock the door again, so we can —"

"Say!" Bill stopped and looked up at me with the beginning of a fierce grin. It was just the sort of trick that would appeal to him. "That's an idea!"

The Red Room was at least a known quantity, and with the flashlight to depend on, the thought of returning through that room was not half so frightening as the thought of facing whatever unknown deviltries of Jamie's making might wait for us at the bottom of the circular staircase.

By the time I stopped Bill, we had done another turn or two down the steps, but now he faced around and shot the beam of the flashlight back up the stairs.

"Okay, let's —"

A booming blast of sound reverberated down the spiral walls around us. Once again, someone had opened the door of the Red Room, but this time with a crash. Bill snapped off the light as we froze, listening.

This time the footsteps were heavy and slow, and with each footstep went a hard metallic clank. Stories of ghastly figures dragging chains rushed into my mind, but in the same instant I knew this was not the clattery sound of chains. This was different.

With Bill but a single step below me, we were close together with our heads on nearly the same level. In the pitch darkness I could feel his hot breath near my ear as he whispered, "Jamie . . ."

It goes to show what the power of having a flashlight

on your side can do for your courage. Because at once I too was sure it was Jamie we heard. Those footsteps, ponderous as a giant's, were so heavy I could almost see the little monster clumping along in some kind of trick shoes, making his big effort to scare us silly . . .

Clump!

Clump!

Clump! The footsteps crossed the room above us slowly and deliberately.

Clang!

I twitched so violently I nearly lost my balance as metal clashed on the metal of the first step above us. The whole staircase quivered from the impact.

Bill grabbed my arm in a hard grip, and somehow I knew at once what he had in mind. He was going to let Jamie pick his way down a few steps in pitch darkness, then scare the living daylights out of him by suddenly switching on the flashlight. I could feel his free arm beside me, pointing our secret weapon back up the stairs.

Clang!

Clang!

Clang!

"Yiiiiiiiiii!"

Bill let out a wild yell and hit the switch, all in an instant.

But the flashlight barely glowed!

CLANG!

Around the bend of the stairs above us appeared the

86

blade of a Roman broadsword, thrust into sight at the angle a soldier would carry it in his hand. Light flashed dimly from its cruel point and from the wet red stain along its edge, and then a foot smashed down into sight, a huge foot, and a leg sheathed in armor, and above it a towering figure —

And then the flashlight winked out.

11

I SAID circular staircases are not something you run down two steps at a time, but I was wrong. Or maybe we flew. Maybe panic gave us wings.

All I know is I leaped and slipped and stumbled but somehow kept my feet in that twisting blackness, and that we were screaming with terror, and that our screams spiraled up and down, doubling and redoubling as they reverberated from those circling iron walls, and that we piled up against a flat wall at the bottom, with the footsteps still coming down behind us, clang! clang! clang!

For an instant we lived the nightmare of being trapped there. But in the next instant the wall gave way, swinging out so suddenly we both catapulted into space and sprawled headlong onto a thick carpet.

A section of bookcase swung shut again into the wall behind us, and the clanging footsteps ceased as though they had never been.

We were back in the library, and the lighted lamp was back on the desk. For a moment we both lay where we were, sprawled on the floor, panting or sobbing, I don't know which, but too frightened to move.

Finally Bill managed to roll over and sit up and look around. Once again, the house was as silent as a tomb. And for once, his face was as pale as mine.

"Let's get out of here!"

A moment before, I would have doubted I could ever move again, but now I leaped to my feet. The only reason we remembered to grab our rain gear was because it was right there where we had left it, on the way out. We snatched up hats and slickers, raced across the porch, and shot outside into what was now little more than a drizzle.

Nothing, not even the arbor, made us pause. We sprinted through it recklessly in the darkness, and had passed through without being touched by anything when a thin scream from the direction of the house made us turn and look back.

Through the tunnel of the arbor we could see a small figure that looked like a woman carrying a baby, running through the garden, and glowing with a pale, fuzzy white light. Behind her was a great figure that glowed with the same livid light, a figure with an armored breastplate and legs sheathed in armor and a great broadsword in its hand. And as we watched, the soldier snatched the baby from the woman's arms, and the sword swung down in a glowing arc — and they vanished.

We ran for the gate, pulled it open, and flung ourselves through it.

"He! he! he!"

There, leaning against a tree with his arms folded, stood Jamie, as though waiting for us. And beside him, scratching himself with one hind leg, sat Major.

We stared at them, breathing too hard to speak. Jamie's lips thinned into a torturer's smile, and his dark eyes glittered with insatiable malice as he watched us, and waited. When Bill did find his voice, what he said took my breath away all over again.

"All right, Jamie, you win!"

I could not believe my ears. Did Bill really mean — I should have known better.

"You're the smartest kid I ever met," he went on. "Come on, now, tell me — how did you work it?"

"Work what? You saw ghosts, didn't you?"

"Aw, come on, now!" protested Bill.

For a moment Jamie stared at him incredulously. At first he seemed surprised into something that was close to respect.

"You still don't believe me, do you? You still think it was all a trick."

But then his face hardened into a sort of weary con-

tempt. With a thrust of his narrow shoulder he pushed himself away from the tree.

"Well, you're wrong," he said.

Whistling to Major, he walked toward the gate with his hands stuck in his pockets, and with the big dog waddling along at his heels. But instead of walking to the gate, he shot a last mocking glance back at us, a glance deepset in evil, and veered to one side. They walked straight at the wall, Jamie and Major, and as they did they seemed to shimmer and dissolve and fade into the stones, and were gone. And the ivy faded into a few straggling creepers, and the door faded into battered bare wood with a few flakes of rusty-brownish paint still clinging to its dark surface.

That was when I began to run again.

I ran and ran, with Bill somewhere behind me yelling for me to wait. I might have run till I dropped from exhaustion if I had not slipped on some wet leaves that sent me headlong onto a sodden stretch of grass between the sidewalk and a wall.

The fall knocked out of me what little breath I had left. Gasping and spent, I had only made it to my knees when Bill caught up to me. He stumbled to a stop and flopped down beside me, too winded to care about the wet and the cold.

For a long moment we stared wildly at each other, unable to do more than puff and blow as we sucked air painfully into our heaving lungs. A streetlamp threw its light into Bill's broad face, and I thought that surely, at last, I would see a surrender to terror there, an acceptance of the unacceptable. But no, that familiar expression was back again!

His fanatical belief in facts, his incredible allegiance to rational explanations for everything, had surmounted even this ultimate test. There was a glint of conviction in his eyes, an eager, explaining look, that told me he had found his own answer even before he blurted it out.

"Listen, you dummy, why didn't you stop?" he panted. "I got it all figured out!"

I glared at him.

"What are you talking about?" I knew what I had seen. I had seen the ghost of a boy with the ghost of a dog sitting beside him scratching the ghost of a flea. That was why Jamie Bly lived with ghosts — because he *was* a ghost.

But Bill did his best to demolish all that with one word.

"Hypnotism!"

"What?"

"That little monkey hypnotized us, that's what he did! And that explains everything!"

The notion was cockeyed enough to shake a harsh laugh out of me.

"What do you mean? How could he do that? I'd like to know when he could have —"

"Don't be a dope! If you knew when it happened, you

94

wouldn't be hypnotized! I don't know how he did it, or when, but we're going to read up on hypnotism and we're going to find out," said Bill, glaring *at* me and *through* me with complete determination. "We're going to find Jamie, too, and we're going to get the goods on him. He's dangerous. He ought to be locked up. He hypnotized us, and then he took us into that old house — that same old house — and made us think we were doing all those things."

With a sharp nod he suddenly called up a phrase from his reading.

"The power of suggestion, that's what they call it. The power of suggestion!"

The light of the streetlamp was still full on his face. It made a disturbing Fact stand out sharply. I pointed to his cheek.

"Power of suggestion, my foot! If we were hypnotized, how come you got scratched again?"

Bill's hand darted to his cheek, but he was not checked for long. A twinge of uncertainty, and then he had an answer.

"He must have scratched it when he made us imagine we were running through that arbor."

"Huh!" I tried to sound skeptical, but inwardly I was relieved, and only too glad he had come up with a possible explanation. We got to our feet. Still shaky, but able to breathe again now without every breath hurting my side, I inspected myself. A dozen wet leaves, shiny red and brown, were plastered to my slicker. I had begun to pick them off when suddenly my heart was in my throat.

I had remembered something which, if it *was* a Fact, would change everything.

My lips stiffened as I babbled a question.

"Do you have a flashlight with you?"

Bill's face went blank. This time I had hit home. I saw that I had, and my voice went shrill with fright.

"Don't tell me you didn't have a flashlight, and don't tell me it didn't go dead on us!"

Bill reached into his pocket and pulled out the small flashlight I remembered. His hand was trembling so badly he almost dropped it. For a moment he stared at it in a daze, fumbling with the switch.

And then he did drop it.

Its beam had flashed on, bright and strong.

12

"THERE!"

Belief had flooded back into Bill's face, stronger than ever. His voice shook with exultant relief.

"There! Now do you believe me? Don't tell me now we weren't hypnotized! We just *imagined* I used that flashlight and it went dead! Jamie found out I had it with me, and he worked it in with everything else!"

Almost dancing with joy, he scooped up the flashlight, turned it off, and said, "Let's go!"

He swept me along down the silent street, his head back and his mind teeming with ideas and plans.

"We've got a lot of thinking to do. First of all, we don't say a word about this to anybody," he declared fiercely. "Not a word."

"Ha! If you think I'd tell *my* folks anything, you're

crazy! They think I've got too much imagination as it is. If I told them about tonight, they'd have the doctor over before I knew what hit me!"

"You can bet your boots on that," Bill agreed grimly. "Nobody's going to believe us — until we get the goods on Jamie. It's lucky tomorrow's Saturday; we can come right back up here in the morning and get on his trail. We'll start with that old caretaker —"

"What? Catch me going near him again! Why, he's as nutty as Jamie, and if he saw us again he'd bat our brains out with that ax handle!"

"No, he wouldn't, not if we went at it right. Anyway, we've got to try him, because he knows Jamie, he called him by name."

"That doesn't mean he knows where he lives."

"No, but he might. Well, anyway, besides looking for him we'll go back to that corner where we met Jamie and ask everybody we see if they know where a kid lives who has a bulldog."

"Let's start with them. That's better than fooling around with that old caretaker," I said, still unenthusiastic about straying back within ax-handle range.

"Okay, we'll start with Harkins Way, but if we don't get anywhere there, we'll go look for him. One way or another we'll find out where Jamie lives . . . and then we'll settle his hash!"

We rounded one of those sweeping curves the streets had so many of up on Mount Alban, and ahead of us we could see Marshall Avenue. There it was, with ordinary cars going past full of ordinary people, with everything as commonplace and everyday and secure as could be. The mere sight of these familiar realities affected me like my mother's hand gently shaking my shoulder to wake me from a nightmare. With every step now it became easier to accept Bill's theories.

He had some money with him, so we stopped at a drugstore and restored ourselves with chocolate ice-cream sodas. By that time, as we sat there at the soda fountain, with bright lights and faces we knew around us, with the soda jerk making silly wisecracks for the benefit of a couple of giggling girls eating sundaes, it seemed as if Bill had to be right. It had to be hypnotism, and Jamie Bly was nothing but a sick-minded, dangerous kid.

But then, of all things, Bill woke up next morning with a sniffle, and his mother kept him in bed all weekend. Not until after school Monday were we able to start our search for Jamie Bly. I remember that weekend as a miserable one, because of having to keep our experience to myself, with no one I dared talk to about it around. My family's questions, casual and routine, had to be given routine, noncommittal answers.

"Well, Bruce, how was your Halloweening?"

"It was okay."

"You must have had to spend most of your time getting under cover out of the rain."

"We did."

"It's a shame it had to rain so much," said my mother sympathetically. "I know it must have taken the edge off your fun."

You wait, I thought to myself. You wait till we get the goods on Jamie Bly, and then I'll tell you something.

Bill did not altogether waste the weekend. He checked the telephone book and found no one listed under the name of Bly. He also got hold of a street map, and with its help we worked out the most direct route to Harkins Way.

Monday came, the school day dragged by, and at last we were able to return to that corner and begin our search for Jamie Bly. All along Harkins Way we asked questions of everyone we caught raking leaves out in their yards or coming down their front walks or taking out their garbage, but nobody had ever seen a boy around with a bulldog. One man went even further.

"I've lived in this house all my life and I've never seen a bulldog in this neighborhood," he told us.

By then Bill was growing impatient.

"Listen, our best bet is that caretaker. We can always come back here if we don't get anywhere with him, but we've got to at least try. For all we know, Jamie may not live anywhere near here. Maybe that's why he picked this corner to meet us on."

"Well . . ."

"Aw, stop worrying. That old guy can't hurt us. We'll keep our distance, and we can always outrun him. The only thing is . . ."

"Is what?"

Bill gave me an odd look, and decided to keep his reservations to himself.

"Never mind. We'll see."

He consulted his street map and piloted us to Beardsley Way. When we got there, we found that Jamie had told at least one truth. A big crew of men were at work around the old, boarded-up house, getting ready to tear it down. The driveway gates were open, but an old man — not the caretaker — was standing guard, waving trucks through and keeping everything and everyone else out. Bill went straight up to him.

"Say, mister, can you tell us where the caretaker is?"

"What caretaker, sonny?"

"The one who looked after this house."

The old man stared down at us.

"Sure, I'll tell you where he is; he's six feet under. The last caretaker this place had died more than a year ago after they carted him off to the booby hatch."

"Oh."

Bill turned away and grinned at my frightened face.

"Might have known it," he said in a low voice, as we stood off to one side. "He hypnotized us twice. The first time was up there in the hall. He made us think that caretaker was down there. When he found that worked, he knew he could really have fun with us that night."

This, I realized, was the possibility that had occurred to Bill when he acted so funny a few minutes earlier,

when we were still over on Harkins Way. Could it be true?

"But . . ." I began, and then stopped, because another man had joined the guard at the gate and they were talking about the house.

"I can remember this place when I was a boy, and even then we was afraid to walk past it," the guard was saying with a reminiscent chuckle. "There was a fire once that burned a big porch off the side of it, and there was stories of bodies found in the ashes, a boy's and a dog's, and there was talk of a baby's body buried in the garden, but it was all hushed up. The old Bly place, we called it then . . ."

We walked away in a dead silence that lasted till Bill finally managed to mutter through stiff lips, "Well, Jamie could have known all that, and that's why he would say his name was Bly . . ."

But we never found Jamie, and gradually we realized we were trapped with our secret. By then, of course, some little time had passed, and the passing of time made it easier to live with. After a while the only reminder we had left of that night was the little scar on Bill's cheek. Long after all signs of the first scratch had disappeared, a small white scar still marked the place where Jamie, or something else, had drawn blood.

I was nearly a grown man before I told my parents about that night. Of course, you can guess how I told the story — disparagingly, making fun of it — and the way my parents received it — their side glances at each other, and their comments concerning the wild imagination I had when I was a boy. If I had been in their place, I would probably have reacted the same way — but I wasn't. I was the one who met the boy who lived with ghosts, and I still don't know what to think about it.